MORE Things to Draw at The Lake

Lydia and Chuck sparring

Roland and me sparring

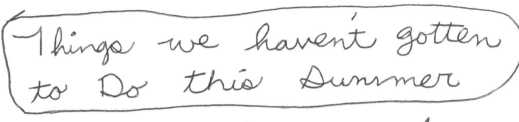

Things we haven't gotten to Do this Summer

① Go on Gretchen's boat.

That's not exactly Gretchen's fault.

Birgit swore that she was going to take us out today, but I guess she forgot. Again.

Sukie's new haircut

More Things we haven't gotten to Do this Summer

② Enroll Julie in Eskrima class!

No thank you, I'll (stick) to Field Hockey.

You said "stick," which means that you like sticks, so you should try stick-fighting.

Or I could just use my field hockey stick—

Sticking my tongue out at you!

Only one more month until

JUNIOR HIGH!

My mom called a family meeting for tonight. I bet she's going to tell Melody and me what we can spend on new clothing and supplies like she does every year.

The yearly budget conversation

You girls need to learn the value of money, so we're going to budget for what you NEED, not what you WANT, and then we're going to...

Stick to the Budget.

She said I __HAD__ to be there, even if your dads are barbecuing tonight.

No. No. No. No. No. No.
No. No. No. No.

NOOOOOO!!!

WORST NEWS EVER
IN THE HISTORY OF
EVER!!! six

WHOLE

Months!!!

Girls, I've been given the most amazing opportunity and it's going to change our lives for six months. My company wants to send me to work on a project in the United Kingdom, in London. We're moving!

TERRIBLE, SHOCKING FACTS ABOUT ENGLAND!

① They spell things differently! My teachers are going to think I'm stupid!

②. The temperature only rises to 32 degrees In The Summer!

③. They're probably going to hate me because they're still mad about us winning the Revolutionary War!!

Do you hate me?

Yes.

④ They eat something called "treacle" and I DON'T KNOW WHAT THAT IS!

⑤ Melody says we're going to be living in a neighborhood where some of Jack the Ripper's victims **MIGHT BE BURIED.** I don't know who Jack the Ripper is, but he sounds bad ('cause ripping stuff is usually bad) (also having victims is usually a sign of badness).

THINGS LYDIA IS SICK of HEARING

It will be great for us to get a Fresh Start!

English accents are hyper super cute!

Just so you know, Black Pudding isn't pudding, it's a sausage made out of blood.

You know better than to listen to Papa Dad, he makes up stuff to scare us.

I'm still not trying Black Pudding.

Lydia is really upset that after all of our hard work last year to prepare for Hannibal Hamlin Junior High, now she won't get to go. I'm really upset, too. But my dads are going to let me take Daddy's laptop into my room for an hour every night, and Mrs. Goldblatt says that she's going to buy a computer for Lydia and Melody to share. Papa Dad even set up accounts so we can chat on the computer.

NEW ONLINE NAMES
I don't know how I feel about my online name, but Papa Dad seemed pretty proud of the names he came up with so I just let it go.
At least mine isn't "Goldbladder."
I don't think our parents would do that to us.
My mom is moving me 6,000 miles away from every-thing I've ever known and loved. There's no telling what she could do next!
Call her own daughter "Goldbladder"?
It could happen.
J LADY BUG ABOO
GOLD STANDARD 3000

There has to be a bright side to this, so I've written a List of Goals —

MY GOALS FOR THIS STUPID MOVE

Goal #1: I have to learn everything I can about London so that I may become Internationally Experienced. While in London I will:

- Use our Time-Tested Strategies for Popularity to Make New Friends

- Become Involved in Sports, or Theater, or, if necessary, Hand-to-Hand Combat (Classes like Eskrima, not actual fighting)

- Not allow anyone to call me Goldbladder

That's reasonable

JULIE'S GOALS FOR THE NEXT 6 MONTHS

To survive the next six months without me, and to continue to gain friends and achieve Popularity so that upon my Victorious Return the two of us will be Hugely Popular.

And I'll have wind in my hair?

SHARED GOAL

To Make Absolutely Certain that Mere Distance won't Destroy our friendship! CHILLING TALE: Daddy used to have a best friend, Judy, in high school, but after she moved to England they never talked again, therefore England has the Potential to Destroy Friendships. BEWARE!

Daddy and Judy a long, long, long, long, long time ago.

PACT

Lydia Goldblatt and Julie Graham-Chang do solemnly swear that despite the fact that Lydia's mom has totally lost her mind and decided to move to a place that is freezing cold and terrible and full of people who rip things, they will update this research journal (kept by Julie) with emails, letters, and scans from Lydia so that it will be like they never separated at all. And the aforementioned Lydia Goldblatt and Julie Graham-Chang will remain friends

NO MATTER WHAT.

Lydia Goldblatt
World Traveler

Julie Graham-Chang
Bookkeeper

Today is the first day without Lydia, and until the Goldblatts are able to hook up their computer I have no idea what she's doing. Papa Dad and Daddy have been trying to comfort me, but nothing works.

JULIE'S GRAPH of MISERY

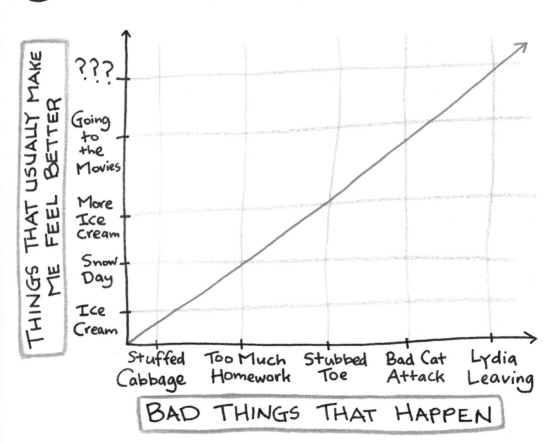

THINGS THAT USUALLY MAKE ME FEEL BETTER

???

Going to the Movies

More Ice Cream

Snow Day

Ice Cream

Stuffed Cabbage · Too Much Homework · Stubbed Toe · Bad Cat Attack · Lydia Leaving

BAD THINGS THAT HAPPEN

Day 0: On The Airplane

The other time that I've been on an airplane was when Mom sent Melody and me to visit Dad in California, so I wasn't scared to go on the plane. Melody was kind of green for the first half hour.

So far I've saved 4 packets of hand sanitizer wipes that + I'm going to send to Julie because she always gives me some when she comes back from a plane trip.

Flying is boooooooring.

Here is your *Moist Towelette.*
It will clean and refresh your hands and face without soap and water. Self dries in seconds, leaving skin smooth and soft.

Directions: Tear open packet, unfold towelette and use.

Made in USA

Qualité

MOIST TOWELETTE

LYDIA'S 1ST EMAIL!

From: goldstandard3000
To: jladybugaboo

It's noon in England but it's 3am at home and we're soooooooo tired. I slept a little on the plane but Mom and Melody were awake the whole time and now they're CRANKY.

There was a driver waiting for us when we got to the airport and he took us to our new "flat." "Flat" is British for "Apartment." There are so many boxes to unpack and Mom says we have to stay awake until 9pm to "get on London time." Melody went out to get coffee. Like she knows where coffee is.

I think I hear Mom snoring. She's already sleeping on the couch!!! England is ridiculous.

THINGS We've Unpacked

1. Sheets and towels
2. Some clothing
3. A frying pan

THINGS WE DON'T HAVE YET

1. Food. I am so tired of eating Indian takeout!!!
2. Curtains. We've been hanging up sheets over the windows.
3. English accents.
4. Friends.

samosas

saag paneer

I have no friends!

5. Artistic ability

I don't need any friends, so I think everything is great!

First chat with Lydia! Yay!

jladybugaboo: I am chatting with you!

goldstandard3000: I am also chatting with you!

jladybugaboo: We are chatting!

goldstandard3000: LOL!

jladybugaboo: What does LOL mean?

goldstandard3000: It means that I am Laughing Out Loud.

jladybugaboo: And why can't you just tell me that something is funny?

goldstandard3000: I just did.

jladybugaboo: This is less like actual talking than I thought it would be.

Just when I thought that the worst was over

Hey Julie, it's Sukie. I just wanted to call to let you know that my aunt is moving my mom and me to New York for a while because there are doctors there who might be able to help her.

So there goes my best friend on the field hockey team. I don't think there's enough ice cream in the world to make this okay.

Actually, this would probably be painfully cold.

HANNIBAL HAMLIN JUNIOR HIGH

I don't have a whole lot of classes with Dee or Maxine or the other field hockey girls, and my classes are all over the school.

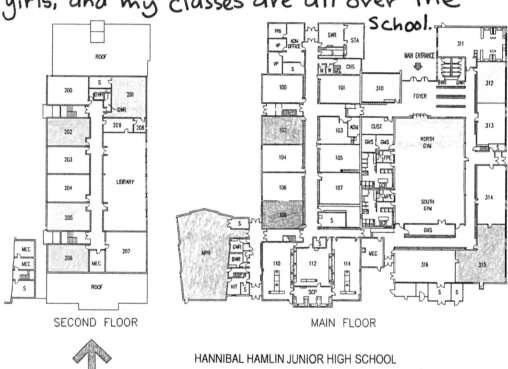

SECOND FLOOR

MAIN FLOOR

HANNIBAL HAMLIN JUNIOR HIGH SCHOOL

N

1. Honors Math
2. English
3. Science
4. Lunch
5. PE/Music
6. Spanish
7. Art
8. Study Hall
9. Social Studies

FIRST DAY of SCHOOL!!!

Math — Easy! And Roland is in my class. He looked confused.

English — We have to read <u>Romeo and Juliet.</u> Boooooooring.

Science — Melody told us last year that we'd have to dissect a moose on our first day. She must have had a different teacher.

Lunch — I didn't feel like eating my lunch at 1Ø:27!! in the morning, and then by 6th period I was so hungry I wanted to eat my chair.

Music — I think I've been put in the class for Kids Who Can't Hold a Tune.

mmm... furniture.

Spanish —The teacher, Señora Weinstein, immediately started talking to me in Spanish as if I already knew it. She didn't try that with anyone else and I felt like a big disappointment when I couldn't understand her, but why would I be taking a Spanish class if I already knew Spanish?

Art — We had to draw a vase of flowers, and the teacher, Ms. Harrington, kept saying

> Draw what you see, not what you think you see!

I thought I did a good job but Ms. Harrington didn't seem convinced.

The rest of my day was pretty easy, except for the business with my locker. I was assigned a locker space that is right between two 8th graders' lockers. The locker on my right belongs to Jonathan Cravens.

Goes by the name of "Jon"

Keeps a skateboard in his locker

Doodles all over his notebooks

goldstandard3000: Are the older kids really cool?

He seems okay. The problem is on my left.

Della Dawn Giampolo

Della Dawn has the locker to my left and she's really intimidating— everyone seems to go out of their way to tell her how nice she looks and how cool her clothing is.

Della Dawn is the Leader of a group of 8th graders who call themselves "the Bichons." It's like a club that everyone wants to be in but no one ever gets invited to join. She kind of ignores me, which is okay, but she opens up her locker all the way so that I have to wait to get into my locker and then I'm late to class.

my locker

Gretchen says that a Bichon Freezay is a kind of a cute dog. Gretchen really, really seems to want to hang out with the Bichons.

A lot.

The BICHONS

Della Dawn Giampolo

Always made-up

The Leader

Jessi Royer

Dresses a lot like Della Dawn

Della Dawn's Second-in-Command

Charmaine Wyatt

Very giggly

Devon Pape

The only Bichon who doesn't seem a little scared of Della Dawn

A boy

Jessi Royer and Devon Pape used to go to Stephen Decatur Senior Elementary School with Lydia and me, but the other Bichons come from other neighborhood schools. There are lots of kids here who I've never seen before, so it's easy for me to imagine what Lydia is going through in London. She must be meeting so many new people! I bet she's already the most popular girl in her school.

THINGS THAT ARE UNFAIR

Melody can go anywhere that she wants because she's "mature." She has **PINK HAIR**!! How is that a sign of maturity? I can only walk by myself for <u>2</u> blocks in each direction from our flat.

jladybugaboo: What are English kids like?

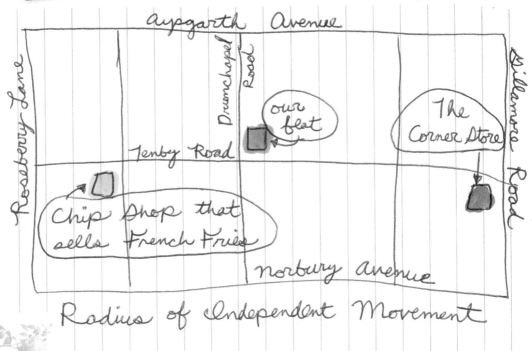

Aysgarth Avenue

Roseberry Lane

Drumchapel Road

our flat

The Corner Store

Willsmore Road

Tenby Road

Chip Shop that sells French Fries

Norbury Avenue

Radius of Independent Movement

From: goldstandard3000
To: jladybugaboo, chuckcavelleri

The craziest thing just happened!

I was wandering around the block when I saw a bunch of big kids circling this little guy, which looked like a bullying situation if ever I saw one, so I jumped in and scared the bullies off with my Superior Fighting Skills!

From: jladybugaboo
To: goldstandard3000

YOU WHAT??????

I didn't really fight the bullies, I just intimidated them with my fighting stance.

But I saved this kids' life! His name is Nabil Waseer and he told me that he's going to be going to the same school as me, which is awesome because I already know someone. We're going to be really good friends once he stops being completely terrified of me.

Eeek! Please avoid killing me!

Nabil ——▶

Chuck's Stupid EMAIL

From: chuckcavelleri
To: goldstandard3000

Remember that Guru Taralanna said that our Eskrima skills should not be used to show off. Be careful over there.

As if I'd show off! I was saving Nabil's life. Chuck is just jealous because he's never had the chance to stand down a large group of bullies.

MORE UNFAIRNESS

Melody has FRIENDS.
School hasn't even started yet
and she already has friends.
How is this possible? They
all look like her. I emailed
Julie and asked her to draw
me a picture of them.

jladybugaboo: Do
they knit?

She's
never seen
them but
I must
have
described
them pretty
well because
they really
look like this.
I miss Julie.

Today Mom and I went to sign me up for school. I told the Headmaster (that's British for "Principal") that I liked being in shows, and she told me that every year in February the students put on a Shakespeare play. Shakespeare never wrote musicals, so I suggested that we throw a couple of songs into this year's production.

What an interesting idea.

She seemed less than sincere.

Lydia gets to wear a School Uniform! How lucky is she? Now she'll never have to worry about what to wear in the morning.

Lydia said that the uniform is green and yellow, so it probably looks something like this

Papa Dad told me that English people really like big hats.

Pants and Sleeves that roll up or down for different weather conditions.

Comfy Sneakers

I have to wear a school uniform! Every day! To School!!!

LAAAAME!!!

stupid Neckerchief →

I always have to wear a skirt! Always!

terrible kneesocks

No trainers! (that means No Sneakers!)

42

I know that if I want to be popular I have to make sure to do some good observing to figure out who the cool kids are so that I don't get trapped with the lame kids, so I'm going to lie low for the first few days and figure out who's cool.

From: goldstandard3000
To: jladybugaboo

There are two girls who are clearly very popular named Victoria and Paulina but I've heard the boys call them by their last names (Ferguson and Gilbert) and girls that are close to them call them by nicknames (Vickers and Pauly) but the girls who aren't friends with them but clearly want to be friends with them call them by their regular first names (or are too afraid to call them anything at all).

I wonder what they'll call me. Maybe Lyds? Or Goldy again, that would be cool.

PROBLEM

I think I waited too long to approach Victoria and Paulina, because today I was approached by Delilah Rigby, who is clearly The Weirdest Girl in School.

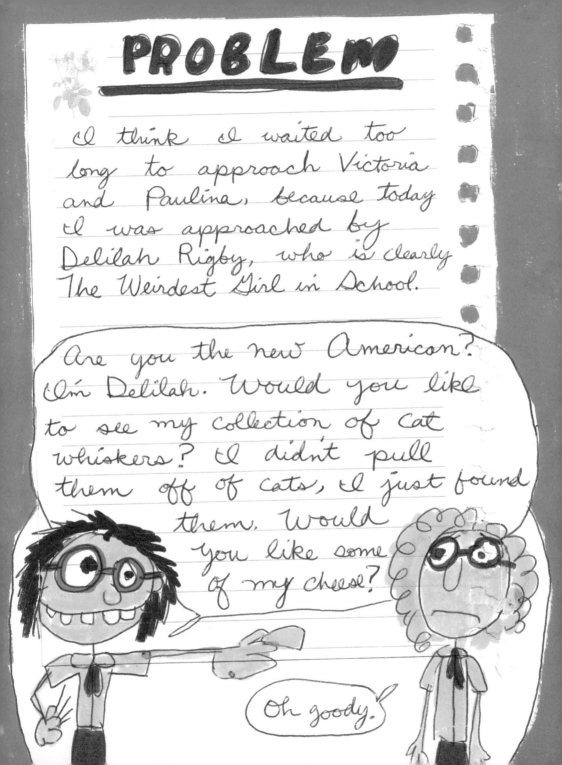

It's weird.
We're all
wearing the
same outfit,
but somehow
Delilah makes hers
look different. I
think she might
be wearing the
skirt inside out.
She has these weird
glasses that are
tinted pink, and
she walks like a giraffe that
has been forced to wear roller
skates (kind of like she's gliding,
but also like she doesn't know
what to do with her neck). I
knew immediately that Delilah
was not the sort of person who
makes new American girls look
cool.

OBSERVATION

Jonathan Cravens seems to be the only person who isn't always telling Della Dawn how great she is. I don't think she likes that, and she seems to try really hard to get him to say something nice.

She'll say

This new lip gloss tastes so yummy!

And he'll say

Okay.

And then she'll seem kind of cranky.

From: jladybugaboo
To: goldstandard3000

You know the boy who has the locker next to mine that I was telling you about? Yesterday he saw some of the drawings that I've been doing for Ms. Harrington's class and he said they were really good! I wish she liked them that much.

From: goldstandard3000
To: jladybugaboo

You should scan them and send them to me, I bet I'll like them.

Weird Thing That Happened Today

I was just minding my own business, waiting to put books in my locker, when all of a sudden Della Dawn started talking to me in a sort of a friendly way. Does this mean that I'm cool now? And how did that happen?

goldstandard3000: I've always thought your shoulders were excellent for holding up your neck.

Della Dawn's Questions

Della Dawn asks a lot of questions. A Lot. Most of them are about Jonathan Cravens.

Did he just look at me?

When he looked at me, did he really look at me?

Was he looking at anyone between 4th and 5th periods?

Was she a blond with kind of a stupid face?

Did Jonathan look like he liked talking to the stupid-faced blond?

She's kind of intense. Still, with Lydia and Sukie gone and Dee busy with Student Government Stuff, it's nice to have a friend.

From: jladybugaboo

To: goldstandard3000

I feel like none of my answers are satisfactory to Della Dawn and I want her to like me because she's a little scary. I wish you were here!

From: goldstandard3000

To: jladybugaboo

I wish I was there, too. Della Dawn sounds so exciting! You have to become better friends with her. If she wants to know more about this Jonathan guy, maybe you should find out more about him! Use your POWERS OF OBSERVATION!

I do have particularly good POWERS of OBSERVATION

Today Ms. Harrington told me

We've got to break You of your Bad Drawing Habits.

which is bad, because I thought I was good at drawing, but good, because Jonathan overheard me talking about it to Roland. He told me not to worry about it because Ms. Harrington only picks On good artists. Della Dawn saw us talking and now She's purposely ignoring me! ???

jladybugaboo: I don't understand why Della Dawn is so mad at me! I thought that she WANTED me to talk to him? Girls are confusing.

goldstandard3000: But we're girls! All we have to do is start thinking like us, and we'll understand them.

jladybugaboo: You're not making any sense!

goldstandard3000: Exactly, and neither are they!

jladybugaboo: WHAT ARE WE TALKING ABOUT???

goldstandard3000: There's no need to shout. Are you going to snog him?

jladybugaboo: What does that mean?

goldstandard3000: I don't know, but they say it all the time here. There are these girls who are always asking me if Nabil and I snog. I think they might know that I don't know what it means. I don't like them very much.

Note to FUTURE SELF

When I'm in 8th grade, I'm going to make a real effort to Make Sense, because the Bichons <u>Do Not.</u> Today Della Dawn was super-friendly to me, as though she hadn't spent the past 3 days totally ignoring me.

Oh my gosh, your overalls are so cute! We're going to Jessi's house after School, you should totally come with.

I was supposed to help Roland with math but I'm Sure he won't mind.

From: jladybugaboo

To: goldstandard3000

Today I hung out with the Bichons at Jessi Royer's house after school! It was mostly weird. I understand maybe half of what they say, because they're always talking about people that I don't know and using words that I don't know. But I think they like me.

Well, at least one of us is doing okay. (Hint: That one of us would **Not** be me.)

Julie

Oh Julie, you're so great and popular!

Julie's cool new friend

From: goldstandard3000
To: jladybugaboo

Guess what! I have a new nickname. The kids here are calling me

THE VIOLENT AMERICAN

I found out from Delilah that my decidedly nonviolent confrontation with the guys who were bullying Nabil is public knowledge, and now everyone at my new school thinks that I'm some sort of bloodthirsty killing machine.

WHICH I AM NOT!!!

From: jladybugaboo
To: goldstandard3000

I think that might be worse than "Goldbladder."

From: goldstandard3000
To: jladybugaboo

YOU THINK?

Violent
←drool

If there's something I learned last year, it's that

Your Friends Are The Coolest People You Know

And Nabil and Delilah are my friends, so therefore they are cool, even if Nabil is scared of everything and Delilah eats banana peels. But weird and Cool are not Mutually Exclusive (which means you can be weird and cool at the same time — look at Melody's new friends).

The peel is good for you!

jladybugaboo: The peel? Really?

So I've decided that I don't need Victoria or Paulina or any of their snooty friends to like me ... I'm out of here in 5 months!

The problem is that Delilah and Nabil have to stay, and I hate the thought of them being picked on after I leave. It probably won't bother Delilah, because she doesn't seem to notice that everyone thinks she's super extra weird, but she still shouldn't be picked on because she's a really nice and friendly super extra weird person.

MISSION:

Nabil and Delilah will have tons of friends by the time I leave!!!

BY AIR MAIL
par avion

Royal Mail®

From: goldstandard3000
To: jladybugaboo

Have you ever heard of "cricket"? It's this game that Nabil loves. It's kind of like baseball if you played it with a canoe oar instead of a bat, and I think that there's only one base but I'm not sure. I'm trying to get Nabil to like soccer instead because it makes more sense, and also everyone here is mad for soccer. Only they call it "Football." Don't even ask.

There's a guy who lives in the neighborhood, Coach Eric, who runs a neighborhood soccer team. I'm totally going to get Nabil to join.

From: jladybugaboo
To: goldstandard3000

I asked Papa Dad why it's called "cricket," and he said it's because the players like to make a chirping sound by rubbing their legs together. I don't think Papa Dad knows anything about cricket.

More Plans!

I think that Delilah might be good at theater (they spell it T-H-E-A-T-R-E here, I don't know why) because she's not really embarrassed by anything and that's a really good quality to have as an actress. Auditions for <u>A Midsummer Night's Dream</u> are coming up, and I think that Delilah would be great in it (and so would I) (even though I tried to read the script and it looked like a gigantic poem, but we'll cross that bridge when we get there).

Hi, I'm William Shakespeare and I wrote a play about a dream that happened in the middle of the summer!

jladybugaboo: Are you nervous?

My collar is very fancy.

Even More Planning

Finally, I've learned from experience that wherever you go, there's probably going to be someone else there who is like you, because if you ended up there, certainly someone who is like you has ended up there as well, and they probably need a friend.

I'm going to find all of the weird kids and bring them together because there is

From: goldstandard3000
To: jladybugaboo

Could you make us a logo?

STRENGTH in NUMBERS

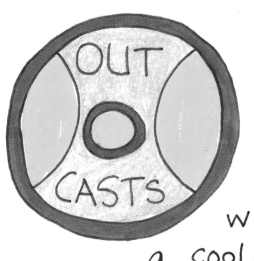

Lydia wanted me to draw a logo for her new group of friends, which is kind of a cool idea, but I wonder what exactly she's going to do with it.

Everyone loves a good tote bag

but the flag might be a little over-the-top.

goldstandard3000: That looks cool! Kind of like a tennis ball, but cooler.

Sometimes I wonder if it's smart to separate yourself from everyone else with a logo or a name — ever since I started spending time with Della Dawn and her friends, other people have been talking about it.

So Devon says I'm a Bichon. Yay?

Papa Dad and Daddy have started to become really, really interested in the Bichons because at least one of them calls me every night, and now my dads want to meet them.

It's Jessi again.

Tell her to come over so we can meet her! Thursday is Stuffed Pepper Night!

And who can resist Stuffed Pepper Night?

From: goldstandard3000
To: jladybugaboo

It's so awesome that you're a Bichon! Congratulations!

I'm not so sure how great it is. The Bichons don't talk to me the way that they talk to each other— they kind of treat me like I'm their pet.

What are you doing?

Drawing.

You are just too cute!

Isn't Jules the cutest?

The total cutest.

They're always saying how "cute" I am.

Daddy pointed out that I am cute, but I don't think that you can trust your dad about cuteness because your dad has to think that you're cute. Papa Dad says that I'm not cute, that I'm a hideous monster beast, but you can't trust Papa Dad because he has no taste. Evidence: last night he put canned corn on homemade pizza.

From: goldstandard3000
To: jladybugaboo

The Outcasts are expanding our ranks! It's not really that difficult to find new members—we just look for the kids who eat lunch by themselves and look miserable, and with a little bit of good old American friendliness, they're in! Nabil mentioned that it might be easy to make friends because lots of kids are scared of me, but I don't think he knows what he's talking about.

I WANT YOU FOR THE OUTCASTS

NEW MEMBER

OUTCASTS

Henry Fortune:

Sci-Fi kid. Has seen every ancient Star Trek episode ever made, as well as every single episode of Buffy the Vampire Slayer.

Can we call ourselves "The Scoobies," like they do on Buffy?

No, we're the Outcasts. We have a logo and everything.

You're like Buffy because you're strong and scary with Martial Arts Skills.

I'm not Scary.

Sure you aren't.

goldstandard3000: The Outcasts have a 5th member!

jladybugaboo: Wow! That was fast. Who is it?

goldstandard3000: This really quiet girl, Becca Gordon. She seems really excited to be part of our crew.

jladybugaboo: How can you tell she's excited if she's really quiet?

goldstandard3000: She's really quietly excited.

jladybugaboo: Oh. It does sound exciting.

goldstandard3000: How are things going with the Bichons? What have you done with them lately?

jladybugaboo: Nothing much. They really like hanging out at the Frost.

goldstandard3000: ??

THINGS BICHONS LIKE to DO

① Go to the Robert Frost Mall
(also known as "the Frost")

When we get there we don't really
do anything. We sit at the fountain
and they talk about the people who
are walking by. Mostly the Bichons
talk about what other people are
wearing and how they probably
shouldn't be wearing that thing. And
then Devon wants to take me shopping
to give me a makeover and I say

No thanks.

One of
these days...

Devon is my favorite but there are limits.

② Go to the skate park. The Bichons don't actually skate but they like to watch other people skate. Mostly Jonathan Cravens.

goldstandard3000:
You should try it!

Today at the skatepark Jonathan offered to teach me how to skateboard, but the Bichons were pretty much against it.

They were really worried that I would get hurt. I guess they really like me.

I feel like the only non-Bichons that I ever talk with anymore (besides Daddy and Papa Dad, who don't count) are Roland and Chuck, and Lydia, I guess. She's so excited about the Bichons that it's hard to tell her that hanging out with them all the time isn't really that fun.

goldstandard3000: Imagine what you could learn! And by the time that I come back, you'll have told them all about me, and we'll both be set for success for the rest of Junior High! We are so lucky.

I wish field hockey tryouts were sooner, but at Hamlin they're not until November.

THINGS the OUTCASTS LIKE to Do

① Eat chips (French Fries). Over here they're served in a paper cone. Delilah puts mayonnaise on hers. Delilah's taste buds are baffling.

chips

②. Practice self-defense moves. I'm the Guru now! Nabil is my best pupil. Henry is no longer allowed to hold weapons.

Henry, after he knocked himself out with his own sticks.

③. Rehearse for Shakespeare auditions!

OW.

BY AIR MAIL
par avion

NEW OBSERVATION

jladybugaboo: Gretchen, Lisa, and Jane have formed their own 6th grade version of the Bichons.

goldstandard3000: Like I'm doing over here with my Outcasts! That's so cool. Are you a member?

jladybugaboo: I don't think that you can be a member of the Bichons and be a member of the Shih-Tzus at the same time.

goldstandard3000: The what?!?

woof!

Shih-Tzus are another kind of little dog that looks like this ➚

Other New Groups at Hamlin

☆ Group of girls from Blossom Valley Elementary. They're the wealthiest kids in town—they have cell phones that can do ANYTHING, and they are always talking about "The Spa." Must investigate what that is. Chuck calls them the Not-So-Awesome Blossoms, but I don't think the nickname is catching on any time soon. Mostly because the Eskrima guys and I are the only ones who have heard it.

Do my science homework.

And brush my hair.

YES MISTRESS

AS YOU WISH

⭐ The Fillmore Elementary Girls. They've been calling themselves "the Fillies," which is a kind of a lady horse. No one messes with the Fillies. I don't know if they want to take the Bichons' place when they leave next year, or if they just don't want to be messed with. There's a rumor that they shoved Jamie Burke into a locker but all us kids from Decatur Elementary know that he just climbed in there himself.

goldstandard3000: I could have told you that.

Still, the Fillies are pretty tough.

PROS and CONS

of Being in a Clique

pros Everyone knows that if they mess with you, they're messing with the whole group, and it's sort of nice to be protected.

There's always someone to talk with on the phone.

LOCKER ACCESS IS GOOD! The Book

It's easy to get things in and out of your locker.

goldstandard3000: And you're automatically cool.

Cons Sometimes you feel like you can't talk with anyone else who isn't in the group.

You don't always want to do what everyone else is doing but you still kind of feel like you have to.

Let's go to the skatepark!

BIG CON

Some of the leaders of the clique can get kind of bossy.

Get me a Diet Cola from the vending machine? Thanks.

You definitely have to never wear that shirt ever again. Ever.

Can you find out if Jonathan is going to the skatepark after school? Thanks.

From: goldstandard3000
To: jladybugaboo

You are so lucky that you're in with the Bichons. As the leader of the Outcasts I have to do so much work to make my friends happy. It's a lot of work. **BUT...**

Nabil is on the Sockball team! I just can't call soccer "football" so I call it Sockball, which really annoys Eric (the sockball coach).

It's called Football.

Then what do you call real football?

American Football.

If you can make up names for stuff then I can, too. Sockball!

From: goldstandard3000
To: jladybugaboo

Nabil almost didn't make the team, but I started talking to Eric and telling him how great Nabil would be with just a little practice, and he believed me. I should be a sports agent. Then we had a conversation about how Melody and Mom and I just moved here from the U.S. and he said that he would love to come by and welcome us properly to the neighborhood. Maybe he'll bring us a pie or a fruit basket. That would be nice.

From: jladybugaboo
To: goldstandard3000

What if he brings you Black Pudding?

From: goldstandard3000
To: jladybugaboo

I forgot to tell you! Papa Dad wasn't lying! Black Pudding is real!!! I haven't tried it. Melody almost fainted when she saw it on the menu at the chip shop.

Field Hockey Tryouts!

I'm so excited to be finally trying out. Dee said that she and Maxine are going to be there and it's going to be great to be on a team with them again. I didn't think I'd miss it so much but I really do.

Field Hockey = HAPPY!

goldstandard3000: BE AGGRESSIVE! B-E AGGRESSIVE! Break a leg!

I didn't make the team.

I can't believe that I didn't make the team.

There were all these much, much bigger girls there, and they were all stronger and faster and way, way more aggressive than me. Maxine and Dee made the team (probably because they're also bigger and faster and more aggressive). I feel like a loser.

From: goldstandard3000
To: jladybugaboo

I can't believe that you didn't make the team. Clearly, the coach is secretly working for a rival school and wants to take down the Hannibal Hamlin team from the inside by dismissing the best players. This is a complete injustice.

The Outcasts would never stand for such treatment! You know, there's been a real drop in bullying ever since The Outcasts were formed. I think I'm doing good work over here. With your in-depth Bichon research and my newfound leadership skills, we'll definitely be set for when I come home, and who will need the field hockey team then?

Oh, also, I'm knitting all the Outcasts scarves. I bet no one on the field hockey team has a scarf made by me. So there.

Now whenever I see Max and Dee they're surrounded by their new Field Hockey Friends.

Thank goodness for Roland and Chuck, even if all Chuck ever talks about any more is Lydia.

So... this guy, Nabil, that Lydia's friends with... is he her really good friend?

Like, on a scale of 1 to 5, how good a friend is he?

jladybugaboo: Roland keeps coming in to school with new scrapes and bruises. I asked him about it but he kept changing the subject and wouldn't give me a straight answer.

goldstandard3000: If someone is bullying him, I'm going to show them what happens to people who mess with my friends!

jladybugaboo: What are you going to show them?

goldstandard3000: Some impressive stick-fighting moves.

jladybugaboo: England is making you scary.

goldstandard3000: I'm not going to beat anyone up, I'm just going to show them that I can beat them up, and then they'll fall in line.

jladybugaboo: I knew that those Kung Fu movies that Chuck kept showing you over the summer were a bad idea.

goldstandard3000: Don't worry, I know what I'm doing.

jladybugaboo: I've heard that one before.

When I got home from hanging out at the Frost with the Bichons, Papa Dad and Daddy asked me to come to the den for a family meeting.

We have something important to tell you.

jladybugaboo: OH MY GOD OH MY GOD OH MY GOD ARE YOU ONLINE PLEASE BE ONLINE I HAVE TO TELL YOU SOMETHING!!!!

goldstandard3000: I'm here I'm here, what?

jladybugaboo: WE'RE COMING TO VISIT!!!!

goldstandard3000: WHAT?????????????

jladybugaboo: PAPA DAD AND DADDY AND I ARE COMING TO VISIT FOR WINTER BREAK!!!!!!!!

goldstandard3000: OH MY GOD OH MY GOD OH MY GOD!!!!!

I can't believe that Julie is going to be here in a month! And Melody and Mom knew all about it and were able to keep a secret from me!

shh!

Ha Ha

This would explain all the sprucing up that Mom has been doing around the flat. I didn't understand why she cared how it looked, seeing how the only guest that we ever have is Coach Eric but now that Julie and her dads are coming I can totally see why she wants everything to be nice.

Clean these ragged edges!

Having to wait a whole month when I know that I'm going to see the Goldblatts is **DESTROYING ME!** Lydia is going to want to know all about everything that's been going on here, so I'm going to the school play auditions so that she knows all about her competition for next year.

I will <u>NOT</u> be auditioning, just watching.

PARTICIPATING

Duh

Help?

OBSERVING

Doo de doo!

JUNIOR HIGH MUSICAL AUDITIONS

Oh my gosh, I feel so terrible for Jane Astley. She got a part originally meant for a boy. Her mom was there and she was Not Happy about it.

And then Jane

FREAKED OUT

jladybugaboo: She said that she was never going to go out for a show again!

goldstandard3000: That's great! When I come back I'll have a much better chance of getting a lead role!

jladybugaboo: I don't know if she meant it. I think that she was just trying to get her mother to leave her alone.

I'm totally going to tell this story to the Outcasts so when they audition for the school play they feel good about the fact that they're doing it because they want to, not because someone is telling them to. There really is a lesson in everything.

There's no way that my Outcasts aren't going to rock the <u>Midsummer Nights' Dream</u> auditions — I've totally trained them how to act.

Just remember to project! Be loud and speak clearly!

What's a Hippolyta?

As long as you're loud and clear it doesn't matter what you're saying. Now say it once more, with feeling!

Shakespearean actors always hold skulls.

NOT PARTICULARLY GOOD THING THAT Happened at AUDITIONS

So it turns out that when Becca gets nervous, she stutters. I hadn't ever noticed it before, but when she got up for her audition, she tried to read the script and it was

AWFUL.

Maybe I shouldn't have pushed her to audition.

Still, it was a learning experience.

When I found Becca I
told her about the time that
I freaked out and sang the
Mattress Kingdom song for
my audition. I think it
cheered her up.

The good news is that
I got the part of Titania!
She's the Queen of the Fairies.
Henry is going to be
Lysander. And Nabil is a
character called "Snug".
And Delilah and maybe
Becca are going to help
with the sets and the
costumes.

Unfortunately Victoria is
going to be Hermia and Paulina
is going to be Helena. They're
the two romantic leads.

But I'd rather be
Titania, because she's the QUEEN

From: jladybugaboo
To: goldstandard3000

So what happens in A Midsummer Night's Dream?

From: goldstandard3000
To: jladybugaboo

Lysander loves Hermia, and Hermia loves Lysander, but Hermia's dad wants her to marry Demetrius, and Helena loves Demetrius, so they all run into a magical forest, where Puck, who is a servant to the King of the Fairies, makes Titania (that's me) fall in love with a guy who has been turned into a donkey. Then Puck makes both Lysander and Demetrius fall in love with Helena, who freaks out, and they all have a fight. And then everyone watches a play. And at one point everyone falls asleep and wakes up to find that everything is okay.

From: jladybugaboo
To: goldstandard3000

?!?

From: goldstandard3000
To: jladybugaboo

Shakespeare is complicated.

Rehearsals aren't as fun as I thought they were going to be. It's nice that Henry and Nabil are there with me, but Victoria and Paulina need a lesson on Not Being Nasty.

These are the forgeries of jealousy

Her accent is atrocious!

But it doesn't matter, because I have my friends and I don't care what snotty girls think about me. I think I've really grown since last year.

Thank goodness it's only ten more days until we leave for England. Della Dawn and the Bichons have started to pick on Chuck.

They always say that they're "just kidding" when they say mean things, but it never really feels like they're kidding. It feels kind of uncomfortable.

Jessi and Charmaine are always asking if Chuck is my boyfriend, and when I say, "No," they say, "You are so cute!" Devon offered to give Chuck a makeover, but I don't know if he was being friendly or mean. I need a break from them.

Okay...weird. As I was leaving school today I found out that

CHUCK HAS BEEN HANGING OUT WITH...JANE?

I guess he was tired of the Bichons making fun of him so he wants to hang out with someone else, but...Jane?

I don't know how long it's been going on but I've noticed that Jane's style has become a lot less...frilly.

Lydia was right, a lot can change in less than a year. I wonder if Jane is taking Eskrima classes. I hope not. I don't want for Lydia to have an excuse to go all ninja on Jane when she comes home. Maybe I just won't mention this to her.

PACKING for LONDON

THE LIST

2 pairs of jeans
1 skirt that the dads are making me bring
1 pair of overalls
2 sweaters
5 shirts
enough underwear for a week
Boots
Warm socks
journal
pens
Colored pencils
markers
eraser
Pencils
Pencil sharpener
glue
a toothbrush

Daddy and Papa Dad are getting really excited for the trip. Papa Dad wants to bring all of his guidebooks and Daddy is kind of freaking out about it.

We are not paying overweight fees on your luggage so that you can bring eight guidebooks!

But they all contain different information!

This one is from 1972! How is this useful?

The pictures are funny.

We leave tomorrow! The Bichons told me that they're going to miss me. They got kind of dramatic about it.

Oh my gosh, I'm going to miss you so much, don't go Li'l Jules!

Bring me back something cool and British.

mrph

goldstandard3000: You're almost here!

By this time tomorrow, the Graham-Changs are going to be here! I think that even Melody is excited.

Or as excited as Melody gets. And I've totally prepared The Outcasts for Julie — she's going to be so impressed with them.

Say "toilet" instead of "bog" and "French Fries" instead of "chips" and "chips" instead of "crisps" so that Julie doesn't get confused.

You're barmy.

Say "crazy".

As soon as Coach Eric drops off his air mattress, we'll be ready!

109

London Bound!!

3 pm We are all packed and ready to go! But the car isn't coming to pick us up until 4:30.

3:45 Daddy can't remember if he packed his travel mouthwash and now he's unpacking his whole bag even though Papa Dad just pointed out that we can always buy some in London.

3:57 Daddy found his mouthwash and is repacking his whole bag.

4:02 Papa Dad is making Daddy some tea to calm him down even though Daddy insists that he's FINE.

4:21 Daddy is staring out the window and waiting for the car to arrive. I don't think the tea is working.

Your dad can be a bit of a nervous traveler.

Papa Dad suggested that I keep a running tally of every time that Daddy freaks out over the course of our trip to London. So far he's freaked out seven times.

"Where is it?!?"

#3: Daddy forgot that Papa Dad was carrying all of our passports.

#4: Papa Dad kept joking about his "Titanium Super-Bionic Pinkie Toe that Shoots Lasers" when he couldn't get through the metal detector without it going off.

NOT FUNNY.

"Don't blame me if the plane leaves without you!!"

#5: Papa Dad and I wanted to look around the airport shops instead of waiting at the gate.

FIRST DAY IN ENGLAND!

We're off to see London and I get to leave the Radius of Independent Movement!

But first... the Chip Shop!

So Devon wants me to bring him back something cool.

Like what?

I don't know. What's cool?

I thought you were supposed to be learning about that from the Bichons!

They're confusing.

Blimey.

Now you're confusing.

Today we went to see the TOWER of LONDON. We saw...

Allo.

A Beefeater

A Fisheater

It's a delicacy!

Crown Jewels

This did not actually happen

Everything was behind really thick glass.

the EXECUTIONER'S BLOCK

That's where the head goes!

It's so great to see you and your dads again — it feels like everything is back to normal, even though we're still in London, and everything is still not normal.

It is not normal to drive on the wrong side of the road.

You get used to it.

Today the dads and I are going to have afternoon tea with Daddy's old friend Judy.

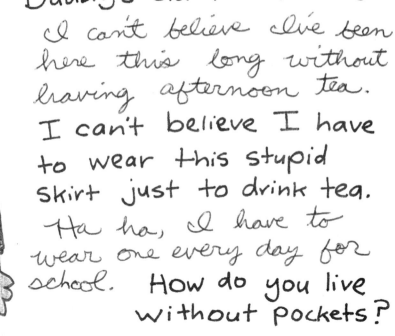

I can't believe I've been here this long without having afternoon tea.

I can't believe I have to wear this stupid skirt just to drink tea.

Ha ha, I have to wear one every day for school. How do you live without pockets?

Afternoon Tea

Papa Dad, Daddy, and I took the Tube (that's British for "subway") into the center of London to meet Judy. She "remembers" me from baby pictures.

> Oh my dear, what a proper little lady you've become!

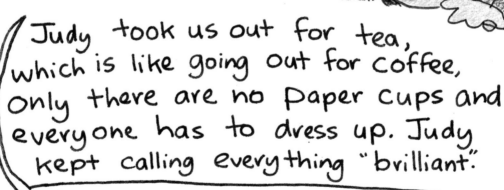

Judy took us out for tea, which is like going out for coffee, only there are no paper cups and everyone has to dress up. Judy kept calling everything "brilliant."

> Darling, you must have a scone, they're brilliant!

Judy liked talking. A lot. Things that Judy talked about (a lot):

1. How grown-up I am.
2. How "adorably plump" Daddy is.
3. How she Never Imagined that Daddy would end up living in "The Burbs."

> And you have a little vegetable garden? Brilliant!

4. How she had dinner with "a Royal."

> It was brilliant!

5. How great her brilliant job is.
6. How she's not currently dating.

> But us single girls prefer our freedom, don't we!

Judy is exhausting.

Papa Dad and I have developed very accurate Judy impressions.

Don't you just adore this tea?

And my tie?

Brilliant!

Also Brilliant!

Oh, and did I mention that yesterday I was crowned the Queen of England?

Brilliantly brilliant!

Let me know when you two are finished.

She seemed a lot cooler back when she and Daddy used to be friends. I _need_ to get out of here. The last thing I want is to turn into a prat like Judy. What's a prat?

Goldblatt/Graham-Chang TRIP to BATH

Right now we're on a train to Bath, the cleanest town in England!

Ha ha. Mom says Bath is an Area of Outstanding Natural Beauty. Officially.

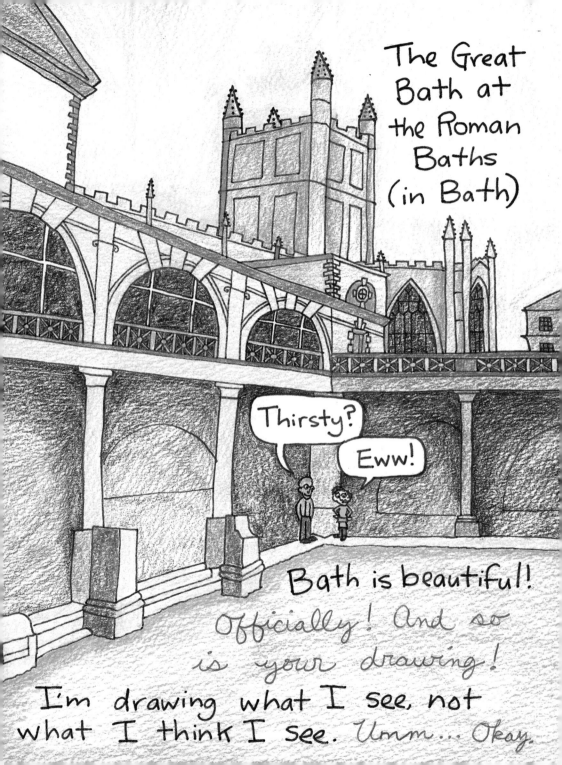

We also went to the Costume Museum, which was excellent.

Today Papa Dad, Daddy, Mrs. Goldblatt, and Coach Eric are going to the British Museum. They were going to take us but Lydia wanted to stay home so I could meet the Outcasts. Daddy said he'd bring us back something cool. I wonder if what he thinks is cool is the same as what Devon would think is cool.

Example: When Daddy went to the Philadelphia Museum of Art last year, he brought me Juggling Monkeys.

Are Juggling Monkeys cool?

Can Devon juggle?

Maybe he would if he had monkeys.

We all went to the chip shop and then Lydia made the Outcasts act out scenes from their play.

What's a votress? A waitress that votes.
Oh.

3:14AM! I <u>still</u> have jet lag and Lydia is snoring, and I can't stop thinking about the way that she talks to the Outcasts. It reminds me of the way that Della Dawn talks to me and the rest of the Bichons. When I mentioned this to Lydia she seemed to think it was a *good* thing.

That's great! I think I'm becoming a really good leader!

But I don't think she understands that I don't think I like the way that Della Dawn talks to me and the rest of the Bichons.

It's great having Julie here, but she's starting to get on my nerves. She's always asking Henry and the others if they really want to be in Midsummer Night's Dream.

You know, if you don't want to go onstage, you don't have to go onstage, it's your choice, blah blah blah.

It's like Julie thinks that she can tell my friends what they can and can't do. I think that being a Bichon has given her a big head.

Waking up at 4 am is _lame._

I don't think that Henry wants to be in the play. He doesn't seem interested in it _at all_. Lydia is being pushy again. I'm beginning to think that being popular just means that you can make other people do what you want them to do. Which I guess is probably why people want to be popular.

Do my bidding!

But I don't want to tell people what to do, so does that mean that I don't want to actually be popular?

PRIVATE

Today we all went to the National Gallery, which had a lot of art. A lot of art. A lot a lot a lot of art. Melody told me that you can see too much art. It's called "Museum Fatigue."

Why doesn't anyone ever try to give us "Ice Cream Fatigue"?

MIDPOINT MEETING

So I've learned how to think Outside the Box when it comes to popularity. Who would have thought I'd end up as the leader of the Outcasts, and you would be a Bichon.

I didn't even know what a Bichon was. Now everyone back home knows who you are, and everyone here knows who I am, and that's what matters. Yay us!

But everyone knows who the Wicked Witch of the West is. I don't think that being well-known is the same as being well-liked. Who wouldn't like us?

We found The Coolest Thing.
It's pretty cool.
They have chocolate eggs over here,
and when you break them, there's
a plastic yellow yolk inside.
And inside the yolk there's a toy
that you've got to put together.

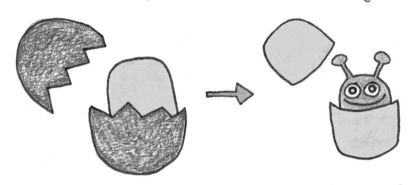

Even Melody thinks it's cool. I'm
going to get a bunch for everyone
back home.

That's
kind of
cool.

my new
scarf!

Handmade!

Today we're going home! It's sad to say good-bye to the Goldblatt Girls (that's what Coach Eric calls Lydia, Melody, and Mrs. Goldblatt) but it's kind of a relief to be going home where everything is familiar and I don't have to sleep on an air mattress.

133

It's good to be back, even if maybe Bad Cat missed us a little too much and won't leave us alone.

She is refusing to get off me.

mrow!

Bad cat.

Now that I'm home, I'm starting to wonder what Lydia will be like when she gets home. She's really used to telling people what to do. What if she turns into Della Dawn? Or Judy?

Friends no matter what, right?

It's so much quieter around the flat now that the Graham-Changs are gone. Julie annoyed me a little but I already miss her. It's going to be great to go back to the States and have everything go back to normal.

Roland

me!

Chuck

Julie

I hope that the Bichons like the chocolate eggs.

NEW YEAR'S EVE

It's now 9 o'clock, and Lydia has been in a totally different year than me for two whole hours. She's **IN THE FUTURE**

I don't like this.

I don't know if Devon liked his chocolate egg.

Oh, how cute! It's exactly what you wanted, isn't it, Devon?

Umm... yes. Thank you, Li'l Jules.

But Roland really liked his, so that was nice.

Oh, we used to have these in Norway!

From: goldstandard3000
To: jladybugaboo

CATASTROPHE!!!!!

I CAUGHT MY MOM SNOGGING COACH ERIC.

Melody doesn't think that it's a big deal, but what if Mom and Coach Eric get married? If she marries him we'll be stuck in London FOREVER and that is NOT PART OF THE PLAN.

From: jladybugaboo
To: goldstandard3000

Wow. That's so weird. Are you sure they were kissing?

From: goldstandard3000
To: jladybugaboo

WHEN A PERSON SMASHES THEIR FACE INTO THE FACE OF ANOTHER PERSON AND THERE ARE SLURPY SOUNDS, THAT'S KISSING.

From: jladybugaboo
To: goldstandard3000

Okay, okay, no need to shout. What are you going to do?

OPERATION BREAKUP

Ideas for Breaking Up Coach Eric and my mom

1. Tell Eric that my mother has a horrible, incurable, yet unromantic disease. All I need is to get something that looks like a medicine bottle and change the label.

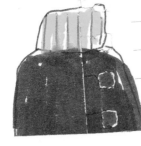

I am ill

For A Horrible, Incurable, Very Unpleasant, Extremely Contagious Disease

2. Tell my mother that Eric once threw a ball directly at Nabil's head. And laughed. Or a cat. Maybe a cat would be better than a ball.

I am an unusually nasty person!

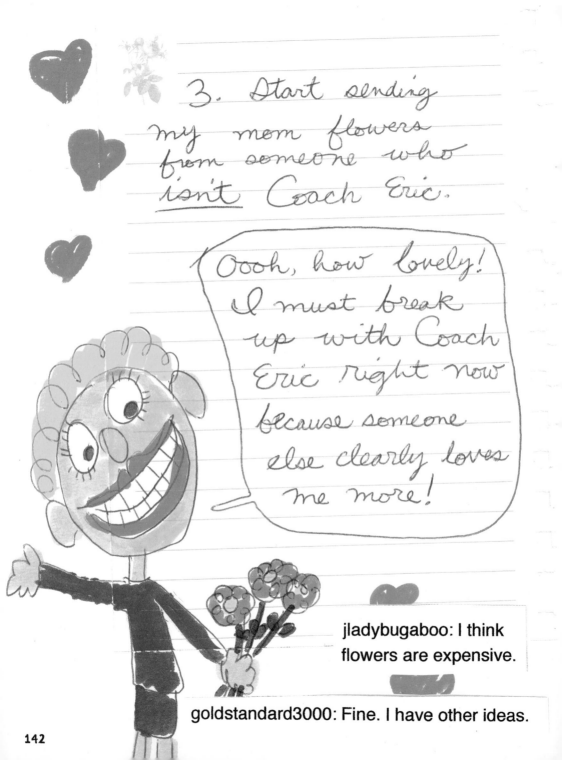

3. Start sending my mom flowers from someone who ~~isn't~~ Coach Eric.

Oooh, how lovely! I must break up with Coach Eric right now because someone else clearly loves me more!

jladybugaboo: I think flowers are expensive.

goldstandard3000: Fine. I have other ideas.

142

4. Become a juvenile delinquent so that my mom <u>has</u> <u>to</u> take me home to the United States where I was a good kid.

me, as a delinquent

I may need some help with this.

When I got back from England I thought about showing my drawings of Bath to Ms. Harrington but she keeps telling me

You're stuck doing what you're comfortable with. You need to try a different approach.

Be different from how you are!

Because right now you're not good enough.

To make matters WORSE, today I found out that Sukie is moving to Manhattan. PERMANENTLY. Lisa told me. Well, she didn't tell me, because she hasn't talked to me since I became a Bichon — She just talked about it really loud as if she wanted me to hear it.

NEW BAD NEWS

Roland is all beat-up again, and now he seems angry at me, as if I was the one who beat him up! What's happening with all of my friends?

Hei Roland...

Friendly, Norwegian greeting

Cranky Norwegian

← Mysterious bruises that he won't talk about

I HATE JUNIOR HIGH!

Clive called an emergency meeting of the Outcasts to help me to become a juvenile delinquent. So far Delilah is the only one of them who has come up with a useful suggestion:

Smoke these!

Cigarettes stolen from Delilah's dad →

But I don't think that I'm a smoking sort of delinquent.

jladybugaboo: You smoked a CIGARETTE?!?

(I tried one and then I barfed.)

BY AIR MAIL
par avion
Royal Mail®

147

The rest of the Outcasts have the _worst_ ideas.

Maybe you ought to have a chat with your Mum about Coach Eric.

This is like when Buffy's sister was acting out. She went on a date with a vampire.

Maybe try smoking again?

Coach Eric is really nice - why don't you like him?

So I asked them

Don't you understand? If Coach Eric marries my mom, I never get to go home and I'll have to stay here forever!

What's wrong with that?

goldstandard3000: Can you believe that they won't help me? Now I'm never going to get back to the States.

jladybugaboo: I don't know why you want to come back to the States at this point. Things are horrible here.

goldstandard3000: That's ridiculous, you're a member of the most popular group in the school.

jladybugaboo: Whatever, you have a bunch of friends who like you so much that they don't want to lose you.

goldstandard3000: They're not going to lose me, I can always chat with them online. Besides, I've given them the tools to succeed, just like I gave you the tools to succeed in Junior High.

jladybugaboo: I'm not successful, I'm miserable! I have no friends, just a bunch of older kids who tell me what to do!

goldstandard3000: They're not telling you what to do, they're teaching you! Just learn and take notes, okay? Learn and improve!

Maybe Lydia is right. Maybe I should take advantage of the time that I have left with the Bichons before they go to high school. Ms. Harrington told me to try different styles, so I'm going to let Devon give me a makeover.

Okay, let's do it.

We've got our work cut out for us, but it could be worse.

How?

I don't know. But I'm sure it could be.

Hey.

Getting a makeover wasn't that bad. We all hung out at Jessi's house and listened to music while everyone made me try on different outfits. I was worried that the Bichons would make me look silly—

But I actually look kind of okay.

I'm a little nervous to go to school tomorrow looking like New Me, but I'm also a little excited.

Today was the first day of being New Me, and even though the shoes that Della Dawn gave me pinch my feet, people seem to like the change.

But Lisa had the weirdest reaction.
Nice outfit.
Thanks.
I never thought you'd be a designer-label girl. Where'd you get the money for those clothes?
My friends gave them to me.
Well, be careful, I don't think they'd like it if you got paint on that shirt.

Oh no no no no no oh no. I asked Devon if I owed him money for the clothing and he laughed at me.

No worries, Jules, I got everything on discount.

Yeah, five-finger discount.

They call it a "five-finger discount" BECAUSE THE FINGERS ARE ON THEIR HANDS THAT THEY USE TO TAKE AND **STEAL** THINGS! I can't wear these clothes. What am I going to do??? **NO ONE CAN KNOW ABOUT THIS.**

If Daddy and Papa Dad find out that I'm a horrible THIEF they're going to be so upset with me!

I can't throw out the clothes because they're really expensive and that would be a horrible waste, but I can't wear them, because they're STOLEN, so for now I have to find a good place to hide them.

But I haven't found a good place yet.

From: goldstandard3000
To: jladybugaboo

Thinking about living in London forever is driving me crazy, and play rehearsals aren't helping. My lines are really difficult to remember. I kind of understand them and I kind of don't. Titania talks about flowers. A lot.

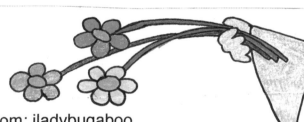

"An odorous chaplet of sweet summer buds, blah blah, etc."

Mom says that Coach Eric is going to come to the play. WHY WOULD HE WANT TO DO THAT?

From: jladybugaboo
To: goldstandard3000

Maybe he loves odorous chaplets of sweet summer buds.

From: goldstandard3000
To: jladybugaboo

Maybe he's going to think my accent is too terrible for London and I should be sent home.

The worst part of all of this is how incredibly _underlined_ unhelpful the Outcasts are being. Henry!!! has been spending most rehearsals hanging out with stupid Victoria and stupid Paulina. I know that his character is supposed to be in love with both of them and it's great that he's making new friends and all, but stupid Victoria and stupid Paulina are still being really snotty to me. I don't think that anyone's ever told Henry about a little thing called **LOYALTY.**

BY AIR MAIL
par avion
Royal Mail®

ow!

This is like when Captain Kirk did something!

I've been thinking that if Coach Eric doesn't come to my play, my mom will say

He doesn't care about the extra-curricular activities of my child!

I must dump him and move back to America right now!!

So I asked Nabil to come up with some sort of sockball emergency on the day of the show so that Coach Eric won't be able to come to the play.

I'm not on the football team anymore. I quit a few weeks ago to join the cricket team.

161

WHY ISN'T ANYONE TELLING ME ANYTHING ANYMORE?

Why would Nabil quit sockball to do a weird sport that nobody's ever heard about that's named after a noisy jumping bug?

---

jladybugaboo: Maybe he did tell you and you weren't listening.

I need to come up with a **NEW PLAN**, because nothing is making sense anymore and smoking half a cigarette and throwing up is not the sort of rebellious thing I have to do if I want to get out of here. I'm going to have to go bigger.

FEBRUARY

It's been a couple of weeks and I don't think that anyone knows that I kind of stole that clothing. Every time that one of the Bichons asks me to go to the Frost I find some sort of excuse to get out of it.

I have a lot of homework.

I have a doctor's appointment.

I have to wash my cat.

I'm filthy.

I'm an international super-spy and I have to be in Ulan Bator by four.

The Bichons thought that Jane and Chuck kissing was the funniest thing in the world. Later on, when the Shih-Tzus walked by, the Bichons teased Jane. To her face!

But then Gretchen said

Whatever, Della Dawn, at least the guy that Jane likes wants to kiss her, unlike some blue-eyed skateboarders that I know.

Shih-Tzus OUT.

RIGHT TO DELLA DAWN'S FACE.
AND JONATHAN WAS STANDING
RIGHT THERE.

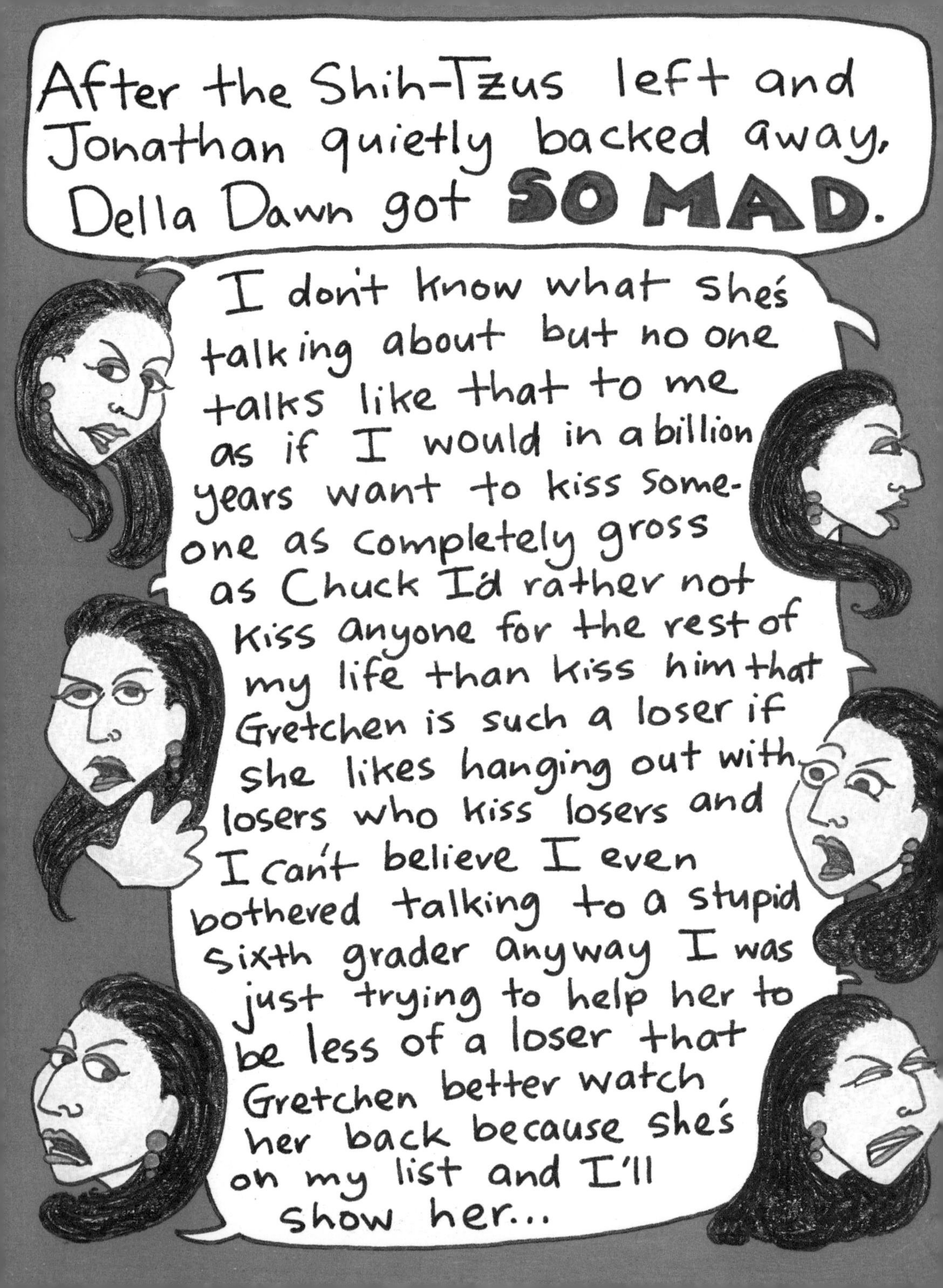
After the Shih-Tzus left and Jonathan quietly backed away, Della Dawn got SO MAD.
I don't know what she's talking about but no one talks like that to me as if I would in a billion years want to kiss some-one as completely gross as Chuck I'd rather not kiss anyone for the rest of my life than kiss him that Gretchen is such a loser if she likes hanging out with losers who kiss losers and I can't believe I even bothered talking to a stupid sixth grader anyway I was just trying to help her to be less of a loser that Gretchen better watch her back because she's on my list and I'll show her...

I've been thinking about how Lydia wants me to learn from the Bichons, and I think I have. I've learned that Della Dawn is mean and Jessi says mean things because she wants to be like Della Dawn and Devon steals stuff and Charmaine just giggles a lot and I don't think that one of them would stand up for me the way that Gretchen stood up for Jane.

Lydia is going to be upset about it, but I really don't want to hang out with the Bichons anymore. She'll be mad, but we promised we'd be friends no matter what, right?

What did you do??

I leave you alone for six months and you become a friendless loser?

If someone is a jerk, they're not going to be my friend. No matter what.

THE PROBLEM WITH BREAKING UP WITH THE BICHONS:

They won't take No for an answer!
All of my excuses for not wanting
to hang out with them are lame,
and they know it. How am I
supposed to get away from them?

I have to find a way for them not to like me.

THE PLAN

I need an expert — Somebody who goes out of their way to make people not like them.

MELODY

I hope she doesn't make me dress up like her, but at this point, I might.

From: jladybugaboo
To: myansweris42

Dear Melody,

Hi! It's Julie. It was nice to see you over the winter holiday. Do you remember when I was talking about the Bichons? You rolled your eyes a lot and called them "gits." I don't know what that meant, but I'm going to assume that it was bad. So I think that I don't want to hang out with them anymore because they boss me around and steal stuff from department stores. Do you have any advice as to how I can make them not like me anymore?

Thanks!

Julie

P.S. There's a spinning wheel in the window of the yarn shop now, and Papa Dad told me that they're going to start keeping a pet sheep inside to save money on wool. You can't always trust what Papa Dad says, but still I did see the spinning wheel and I thought it was neat.

From: myansweris42
To: jladybugaboo

Hey Julie,

"Git" is a British way of saying "jerk." I'll use it in a sentence: Anyone who names themselves after a prissy little dog is a git.

I don't know why you started hanging out with them, but whatever. All you have to do is tell the leader to shove off. Gits like her aren't used to people not falling all over themselves to impress her. Either she'll respect you for standing up to her or she'll hate you forever. It's a win-win situation.

Good luck! The spinning wheel sounds cool, say hi to Margaret and Carol at the yarn shop for me.

Mel

P.S. If telling her to shove off doesn't work, tell the boy that she likes that she has bad breath. There's always a boy.

Melody is still a little terrifying.

Update on
The PLAN to GET OUT of ENGLAND

If I'm going to go big, I'm going to have to make some sacrifices. I've embarrassed myself in public before and if embarrassing myself in public again is what I have to do, I'll do it, and I'll do it by myself because the Outcasts are no longer trustworthy.

Hangs out with Nasty Girls

Unhelpful crickets

Made me barf

WAYS TO CREATE a SCENE

①. Steal something. It would have to be something really, really big.

Lydia never stole elephants back in the United States!

PROS
It would definitely get Mom's attention.

CONS
I don't want to go to jail. So illegal activities are out of the question. For now.

8. RUIN the PLAY

Ways to Sabotage <u>A</u>
<u>Midsummer Night's Dream</u>

a. Find a way to make
myself throw up on stage
(preferably on Victoria
<u>and</u> Paulina).

b. Bring my Eskrima sticks
onto stage and use them to
take out a set piece.

c. Go off script and start
singing something. Maybe
the American National
Anthem.

PROS

It will get
everyone's attention.

CONS

I really don't
want to do it.

From: goldstandard3000
To: jladybugaboo

I've decided to go with Option #3: I'm going to sabotage the play.

From: jladybugaboo
To: goldstandard3000

Don't do it, Lydia. Don't sing the Mattress Kingdom song again.

When you need your Umm Yum Yummy Sleeeep...

Is this Shakespeare?

From: goldstandard3000
To: jladybugaboo

If my mom sees me messing up the play, she'll know that living in London has turned me into a crazy, savage person, and if Coach Eric sees it, he'll know that if he marries my mom, he's going to have a crazy, savage person as a stepdaughter.

Things to do in Maths
PLAN for SABOTAGE

There's a whole section of <u>A Mid-Summer Night's Dream</u> where Titania (that's me) falls asleep. When Hermia (Victoria) and Lysander (Henry) lay down to sleep (there's a lot of sleeping in this play) I'll use the Whoopee Cushion that Henry lent me.

> What is that unearthly odor? I doth believeth that the lady Hermia has farteth tremendously. I am faint with the horror of the stink!

I'll keep using the Whoopee Cushion until they drag me offstage.

PROBLEM.

I lent my maths notebook to Becca during the final dress rehearsal and she found my Plan for Sabotage.

I can't let you do th-th-this! It's n-n-n-not right and you know it and unless you promise not to do it I'll I'll t-t-t-tell someone and you'll be kicked out of the show!

Becca is the one who has been helping me with my lines — she's the only one who could take my place if I was kicked off the show. She'd never be brave enough to do that. Would she?

goldstandard3000: I don't know what to do.

jladybugaboo: Wow, Becca confronted you like that?

goldstandard3000: Yes.

jladybugaboo: That must have been really difficult for her.

goldstandard3000: I know. Now I feel terrible. But I don't want to stay here. I want to come home and not be "The Violent American" anymore.

jladybugaboo: Would it help if I told you that I'm going to tell Della Dawn that I don't want to be friends with her anymore?

goldstandard3000: Ha ha. Very funny.

jladybugaboo: So what are you going to do?

goldstandard3000: I dunno. Something.

If Becca is brave enough to confront Lydia, I can confront Della Dawn. What's the worst thing that could happen to me?

Confrontation is never really on my List of Fun Things to Do.

Today Della Dawn came up to me and said

Wear your new clothes already!

And I said

NO. I DON'T WANT TO.

Ha ha, very funny, Jules.

And then I said

I would rather not hang out with you. The mall is boring, and you're mean, and you steal things, and I don't like it, and if you want to be my friend you're going to have to start doing things that I like, too.

And then I walked away.

And forgot my notebook. And had to go back. It was awkward.

And then I walked away again.

I don't think that I can go through with the Sabotage. It doesn't feel right. Also, Henry asked for his Whoopee Cushion back. My mom noticed that I was unhappy about it.

What's wrong, sweetie? You've been looking really down lately.

So I told her everything. I told her about how I was going to ruin the play because I didn't want to stay in London, and how if she married Coach Eric I'd have to stay and I just really want to go home where no one is snotty to me, and I miss Julie and Chuck and Gretchen, and if Mom had ever bothered to ask me if I ever wanted to live in England, I would have said **NO.**

My Lydia,

I've been thinking about everything that you told me this afternoon, and I want to apologize for never consulting with you about the move to London. I was so excited for the opportunity that I never took your feelings into consideration. That was a big mistake.

I want you to know that no matter what happens, we will be moving back to the U.S. as planned. I hope that you can forgive me for not allowing you to be part of the decision-making process, and I promise never to do it again.

Break a leg! I know you're going to shine tonight because you are and have always been my bright star. Love, Mom

I think that the important thing for everyone to keep in mind is that I really, really didn't mean to sabotage the play. In fact I believe (and the Outcasts agree with me) that I saved the play.

Everything was going fine, until...

Victoria totally forgot her lines. It was completely quiet onstage for about 15 seconds, which is really quite a long time when you think about it.

189

What was I supposed to do?
So, I bet you're really upset that your boyfriend Lysander is gone because he's fallen in love with your buddy Helena. That sucks. Why don't you go and try to find them?
That sounds like a very good plan.
Good girl. I'm going back to sleep. Sooooo sleepy! Sleeping now! Good night!

The director was **SO MAD** at me, like it was my fault.

How dare you defile the words of the Bard!!!

What's a bard?

But then Victoria defended me!

It's not her fault that I messed up! Sure, her accent is terrible, but if it weren't for Lydia I'd still be standing onstage with nothing to say!

So I guess she's not a complete prat.

It's been a couple of days without friends, which isn't that nice. Della Dawn has gone back to pretending I don't exist and blocking my locker.

Papa Dad and Daddy have been asking why I'm not getting phone calls anymore, but I haven't told them anything. At least they still like me. It's probably lame to only have your dads as your friends, but it's better than nothing.

Ms. Harrington liked what I did! She hung my drawing of Papa Dad on the wall outside of the art room, and Jonathan told me that it was great. Then he asked if I wanted to come with him to the skatepark.

And THEN!!!

ROLAND WAS THERE!

Roland has been learning to skateboard! His brother, Pete, has been teaching him. He's not that bad now, although according to Jonathan, he was really bad at first— that's why he was looking so beat-up all the time.

He used to land with his face.

A lot.

So now I'm learning to skateboard. Pete lent me some of his old gear.

Ready to roll?

Standing still on the board is really working for me right now.

It's been really fun to hang out with Roland and Pete.

Well, mostly fun.

Ow.

and ow.

jladybugaboo: I'm learning how to skateboard!

goldstandard3000: That's awesome! The director said I destroyed Shakespeare.

jladybugaboo: Oh no!!!

goldstandard3000: I didn't mean to. But it's going to be okay. And guess who's going to be back in the United States as scheduled?

jladybugaboo: THE GOLDBLATT GIRLS?

goldstandard3000: YES!!

jladybugaboo: YAY!!!!

When I asked Roland why he didn't tell me that he was learning how to skateboard, he was really embarrassed.

I didn't want you to know that I was bad at it.

As if I wouldn't be his friend if he was bad at something! I was almost not his friend because he wouldn't tell me why he was so banged up. I'm going to tell Lydia about what happened with the Bichons. Keeping stuff from your friends is almost the same thing as lying.

Today the Outcasts and I went to see Nabil's cricket match. Victoria and Paulina were there and they sat with us. They've been a lot nicer to me since I saved the play, and I think that one or both of them might like Henry.

Henry seemed happy.

I was totally right
about cricket being completely
confusing.

Blah blah bat, blah blah blah
ball blah blah white pants blah

I'm definitely not going
to miss this. But I
am going to miss all of
them.
Only two more weeks...

The Bichons are still not talking to me, but I kind of get the feeling that Devon wants to. Well, he should be brave and just talk to me. I'll never understand how he can be brave enough to steal things, but saying "Hi" to me is scary. People are weird.

Della Dawn is still blocking my locker, but it's okay because Roland is helping me to carry my books around. Who needs a locker?

goldstandard3000: We're almost totally packed and ready to come home!

jladybugaboo: Yay!

goldstandard3000: Melody and Mom are all sad to leave. I'm a little sad, but I can't wait to see you and Daddy and Papa Dad and meet the Bichons and see Chuck and everyone!

jladybugaboo: Oh. About that. The Bichons totally hate me, the Shih-Tzus mostly hate me, and Chuck is dating Jane Astley.

goldstandard3000: !

goldstandard3000: !!!

jladybugaboo: Are you mad?

goldstandard3000: !!!!!!!!!!!!!!!!!!!!!!!!!!!!

goldstandard3000: !!!!!!!!

jladybugaboo: Are those mad exclamation points?

goldstandard3000: I don't think so. No, I'm not mad. Just excited.

jladybugaboo: Excited for what?

goldstandard3000: Excited for all the planning that we're going to do when I get home! I've learned so much here. First, we're going to start our own crew, and we're going to give it a cool name, and you're going to draw a logo, and maybe we can make up a theme song...

LIST of THINGS to ACCOMPLISH once I GET HOME

1. Take a long walk (farther than two blocks away from the house)
2. Give Julie a hug
3. Eat a burrito
4. Let Bad Cat chew on my arm for old time's sake
5. Pay more attention to Mom's dating activities
6. Start a crew
   ⓐ Us
   ⓑ Chuck
   ⓒ Roland
   ⓓ The Shik-Tyus
   ⓔ The Outcasts (they'll be part of the British division)

Here we go again...

I wonder where we'll go next.

Hey, look, my head is the size of North Africa!

It's good to have you back.

It's nice to be home.

Acknowledgments

I would to thank the wonderful staff at Amulet, who have worked tirelessly to bring this book to the world, specifically Susan Van Metre, Scott Auerbach, Melissa Arnst, Chad W. Beckerman, Regina Castillo, Rob Sternitzky, Laura Mihalick, and the indefatigable Jason Wells. Super extra thanks to my fantastic editor, Maggie Lehrman, whose thoughtful discussion of medieval weaponry is one of my favorite parts of the writing process. Thanks to Avielah Barclay for her knowledge of all things British, even though she is Canadian, and to my zealous friends and family members who have told everyone they've ever met to read my book, particularly my dad, who has no qualms about shouting at his own clients until they buy a copy.

Many, many thanks as always to my champions at Writers House, Dan Lazar and Stephen Barr, and loving gratitude to my favorite redhead of all time, Mark.

About the Author

Amy Ignatow is a cartoonist and the author of
*The Popularity Papers: Research for the Social
Improvement and General Betterment of Lydia Goldblatt
and Julie Graham-Chang*. She is a graduate of Moore
College of Art and Design and is very good at peeling
oranges. Amy lives in Philadelphia with her husband,
Mark, and their cat, Mathilda, who is mostly very terrible.

To my best friend, Mark, the coolest husband I know.
—Ig

Artist's Note: The materials used to create the book are ink, colored pencil, colored marker, yarn, and digital.

Library of Congress Control Number: 2010930192

ISBN: 978-0-8109-9724-0

Text and illustrations copyright © 2011 Amy Ignatow
Book design by Amy Ignatow and Melissa Arnst

Printed and bound in China
10 9 8 7 6 5 4 3 2 1

Amulet Books are available at special discounts when purchased in quantity for premiums and promotions as well as fundraising or educational use. Special editions can also be created to specification. For details, contact specialmarkets@abramsbooks.com or the address below.

ABRAMS
THE ART OF BOOKS SINCE 1949

115 West 18th Street
New York, NY 10011
www.abramsbooks.com